The Cat Who
Came for Tacos

by Diana Star Helmer

Illustrated by Viví Escrivá

Library of Congress Cataloging-in-Publication Data

Helmer, Diana Star, 1962~
The cat who came for tacos / by Diana Star Helmer ; illustrated by
Viví Escrivá.
p. cm.
Summary: When kindly Señor Tomas and Señora Rosa welcome a stray cat
into their home and share tuna tacos with him, insisting that he use
proper table manners, they find that he has a lesson for them, as well.
ISBN 0~8075~5106~6 (hardcover)
[1. Cats—Fiction. 2. Food habits—Fiction. 3. Manners and
customs—Fiction.] I. Escrivá, Viví, ill. II. Title.
PZ7.H3756Cat 2003 [E]—dc21 2003002097

The illustrations were done in watercolor and pencil.
The design is by Carol Gildar.

For more information about Albert Whitman & Company,
please visit our web site at www.albertwhitman.com.

For the real Flynn,
the real Tomás, and their
guardian Angel.
dh

For Andrés, Adrián, Paula, and Julieta.
ve

One moonless night, a cat fell asleep on the steps of a softly lit house.

The cat was still there in the morning, when a woman opened the door.

"¡Hola!" said the woman. "Hello! Where did you come from?"

The cat stood up. Its eyes were wide. Its middle was thin.

A man came to the door. "¡Pobrecito! Poor thing!" he said. "Have you no home?"

The cat looked into their eyes.

At once, the woman said, "Call this home, if you want it. Mi casa es su casa. My home is your home."

"Oh, yes!" said the man. "Please, come in, my friend. Mi casa es su casa. My home is your home."

They held the door open. The cat came in.

The woman said, "Welcome! Please tell us your name."
"Flynn," said the cat.

"Welcome, Flynn," said the man. "This is Señora Rosa.
I am Señor Tomás. And this is your home. Look around!
We'll make lunch."

So Flynn walked through the bedroom . . .the living
room . . . and the bathroom . . .

. . . before he went into the kitchen. The kitchen smelled
fishy. Delicious! Flynn could tell by the smell that this
lunch would be grand!

At last: "Lunch is served!" Oh, what beautiful words!
Señora Rosa and Señor Tomás sat down at the table.
Flynn sat *on* the table.

"¡Mi amigo!" cried Señora Rosa. "My friend! Mi casa es su casa. My home is your home. But in my home, everyone *dresses* for meals. Only those with clothes sit at the table."

Flynn jumped to the floor—and he thought.

Then he went to the bedroom, where he'd seen two dolls. One doll wore a wedding dress. One wore a fine tuxedo.

Flynn took the doll's tuxedo off. He put on the pants. He put on the shirt, the jacket, and the tie.

He went back to the kitchen and jumped on the table.

"¡Qué bien!" Señora Rosa smiled. "How nice! You look so handsome."

Flynn sat by his plate. Señor Tomás coughed.

"Flynn, mi amigo," said Señor Tomás. "Mi casa es su casa. My home is your home. But in my home, people must sit on *chairs* to eat dinner here at the table."

Flynn jumped from the table. He sat on his chair.
Now he couldn't see his plate. He couldn't see the people.
Just the tips of his ears peeked over the table.

So Flynn stood on his chair, with his paws by his plate.
"No elbows on the table," said Señora Rosa.
Flynn sat on the chair — and he thought.

Flynn jumped down again and walked into the living room. He'd seen pillows there on the sofa.

Flynn took a pillow to put on his chair. He sat on the pillow. He was tall enough now — with no elbows on the table!

"¡Muy bien!" said Señor Tomás. "Very nice!"

Señora Rosa picked up the big plate.

Flynn pricked up his whiskers.

But the señora cried, "Flynn, I almost forgot! Mi casa es su casa. My home is your home. But in my home, people must wash their hands before they may eat at the table."

Flynn washed his paws with his tongue every day. He licked his paws now. They were clean.

Señor Tomás smiled. "Please use soap," he said.

Flynn thought soap was sticky and stinky and cold.
But he went to the bathroom and jumped to the sink.

Flynn patted the soap with one paw, then the other. He
didn't get suds on his shiny tuxedo. Flynn rinsed off his
paws, then he licked them both dry.

Flynn went back to his pillow. He straightened his tie.

"¡Qué bien!" The señora beamed. "How nice!"
And she served everyone tuna tacos.
What a fishy, delicious feast!

Señor Tomás whispered, "Flynn! ¡Mi amigo!"

Flynn lifted his face from his plate. He saw that Señor Tomás *held* his taco.

So Flynn picked up his taco, too.

It still tasted better than catnip. Ahhh!

Flynn licked his paws and wiped fish from his whiskers and sighed when his tuna was gone.

Señora Rosa put peas on
his plate.
Flynn sniffed the peas.
He poked one with his paw.

"We use our spoons for
peas," said the señor.
Flynn picked up his spoon
and used that to poke peas.
"Don't play with peas.
Eat them," said Señora Rosa.

But Flynn didn't want to eat squishy green peas.
He covered them up with a napkin.

"Flynn," Señora Rosa sang, "mi casa es su casa. My home is your home. But in *my* home, a person must eat up his peas if he wants chocolate cake for dessert!"

But Flynn was a cat. And cats don't like cake any more than they like squishy peas.

So Flynn jumped from his chair.

He went back to the bedroom, and gave the doll back its
tuxedo — the pants and the shirt and the jacket and the tie.
Then Flynn took his chair pillow back to the sofa.

Finally, Flynn jumped up onto the sofa. He washed lovely
leftover tuna from his toes. He didn't use water and cold
stinky soap. He licked—just the way that cats like to.

Then Flynn stretched out long on the sofa, yawned, and
closed his golden eyes.

He could smell chocolate cake as the two people ate.
He smelled fish again as they washed up the plates.

Then, Flynn heard footsteps come close to the sofa.
He opened his eyes. He saw two people smiling.
"¿Señor Tomás? ¿Señora Rosa?" Flynn asked. "¿Su casa
es mi casa? Your home is my home?"

"Yes, mi amigo, of course," they both said.

"Gracias," Flynn said. "I thank you, my friends. *Mi* casa es *su* casa, too. And in *my* home, you must have a warm, roomy lap if you wish to sit on the sofa."

So Señor Tomás made a warm, roomy lap. Señora Rosa did, too.

Flynn looked from one to the other. "Please — sit closer together," he said.

They did. Flynn stretched across both laps at once.
He closed his eyes.
"Qué bien," Flynn sighed.
And everybody purred.